RADAR
the Rescue Dog

By Janet Love Morrison • **Illustrated by Zuzana Riha Driediger**

With a foreword by Justin Trudeau

Produced by:

FriesenPress
Suite 300 – 852 Fort Street
Victoria, BC, Canada V8W 1H8

www.friesenpress.com

Distributed to the trade by The Ingram Book Company

Acknowledgements

The safety of mountain guests is critical in all ski areas. Much like we are taught about the hazards of water, electricity and fire, we must also teach young people about the fundamentals of mountain safety. This is the intent of Radar the Rescue Dog.

We would like to thank the American Friends of Whistler and Whistler-Blackcomb for their generous financial support.

In addition, thanks to everyone who wrote letters supporting the need to educate and protect young mountain recreationalists.

Foreword

Canadians have always loved to play outside. There's nothing better than challenging yourself to push your own limits by exploring our wild spaces and by exchanging the busyness of our city sidewalks for the majestic peacefulness of our great outdoors.

However, more and more, young Canadians are living enclosed, cocooned by our created spaces. Video games, virtual realities, and online networks are obvious constructs, but so is a hockey arena, a swimming pool, and even a soccer field or a baseball diamond. There is great value in all those, of course, but even greater value beyond, free from frameworks and rule books, marked paths and straight lines.

Our young people need to feel free to wander in the woods, to explore beyond the fences, to measure themselves against the natural world and discover they can hold their own. This is a basic need that, instead of suppressing, we need to shape and direct so that they are empowered to make smart decisions and manage their own risks.

Stories like Radar the Rescue Dog illustrate that poor planning, the wrong gear, or just one bad decision in the wilderness can turn the best day ever into the worst. We need to teach our kids to be prepared and to think things through, as well as to listen to the experts and to people who have more experience.

Teaching kids to take responsibility for their actions, giving them the self-confidence to not be peer-pressured into bad decisions, and allowing them to develop sound judgment in difficult situations are all ways of ensuring that our young people will have the tools to face whatever challenges life throws their way. That's how we protect them, and the conversations that this story will trigger are an important first step.

Justin Trudeau
Leader of the Liberal Party of Canada
MP – Papineau
House of Commons
Ottawa

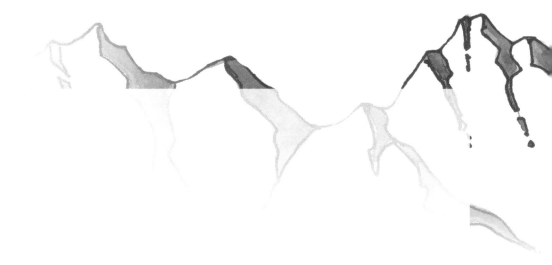

It was a beautiful, early spring morning as Radar and his human pal Bruce left their house and walked down the roads of Whistler, British Columbia.

They were on their way to work.

Radar walked quietly at Bruce's heels. He was a big German shepherd, black all over except for a little tan between his toes. He was wearing his bright orange bib that read, "Canadian Avalanche Rescue Dog Association" on the side. He kept his eyes on Bruce. He and Bruce were a team and Radar was always careful to watch Bruce. He didn't want to miss anything he was told to do.

Bruce looked up at the mountains. He knew about snow and he knew about mountains. Even though the mountains looked so peaceful and everyone would soon be having a great time, Bruce knew that the combination of cold nights and warm days could trigger a skier's worst danger - an avalanche.

As long as skiers stayed within the ski area boundary, they were safe. But some skiers didn't care. They liked to ignore the warning signs to explore the trees, which meant they could be in danger. If something happened, someone would have to rescue them. This was Bruce and Radar's job. They were a rescue team. If someone got lost, or were buried by an avalanche, Radar's keen nose could sniff them out and save them before they ran out of oxygen.

It was still early in the morning and the mountain staff was heading up to work. The ski area would be open soon and skiers would be ascending to the top of the mountain.

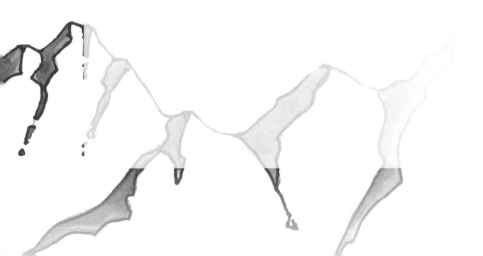

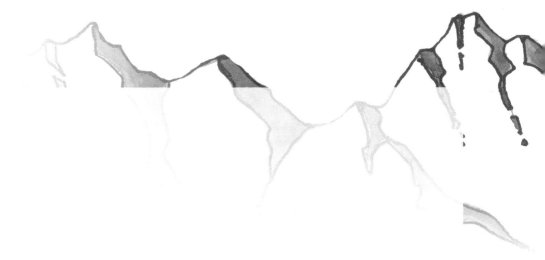

Shortly after, around nine o'clock, a group of children reached the top of the mountain. As they skied off the lift they saw Radar and Bruce, immediately they waved and called, "Hi Radar, hi Bruce!"

Bruce waved back. Radar wagged his tail, but he stood quietly at Bruce's feet.

A young boy skied over to them.

"Hi Bruce, can me and my friends say hello to Radar?"

"Sure," Bruce said. "Just remember, when a dog is wearing an identification bib, the dog is working and the dog's master is trying to keep the dog under control."

Radar sat at Bruce's feet. His black ears were perked, and he watched Bruce's face, ready to do whatever Bruce commanded.

The children gathered around Bruce and Radar. Some of them gently scratched his ears. Some of them patted his head.

"Now remember kids, when you go skiing and snowboarding, it's important to obey the rules. If someone gets lost on the mountain, or caught in an avalanche, Radar is trained to find them. He can smell things much better than you or I can. He can smell people even if they are buried under the snow. Did you know Radar is Canada's first civilian validated avalanche rescue dog?"

"No ..." they said in unison.

"Yes, he is and so he has an important job to do."

"Does he dig people out?" asked one boy.

"No, that's the job of the other members of the rescue team," said Bruce. He continued to explain, "One of the ski patrol's job is to find people who get lost. You kids know you are never supposed to go beyond the boundary markers, right? And remember not to go off into the trees."

"What could happen?" asked a blond girl whose braided golden pigtails stuck out from under her bright yellow helmet.

"You could get lost in the mountains or caught in an avalanche," said Bruce. "These mountains can be very dangerous places. Yesterday we rescued a girl about your age who was caught in a tree well."

"What's a tree well?" she asked.

"It's the loose snow around the tree trunk, the tree's branches shelter the trunk from snow so it's like a well and it can be like a trap if you end upside down in one. You can't get out by yourself. So be very careful and don't get too close to the trees, especially after a snowfall. We want you to come here, have fun and be safe while you're up here."

"What should we do if we see an avalanche?" wondered a smaller, young girl.

"And how do we know if there is going to be an avalanche?" asked another boy.

"Snow can slide down any moderately steep slope. You kids should avoid crossing any un-skied slope all bunched up together. Keep separate by about 12 to 15 metres. If you're ever caught, try to swim like you're in water and try to get rid of your ski poles and other gear, because they will pull you down under the snow. If you feel yourself coming to a stop and you're not on the surface try to put you hands in front of your face to form an air pocket." Bruce put his hands up in front of his face to demonstrate.

"That sounds scary," said the girl with brown hair.

"Just remember to stay inside the ski area boundaries and you'll be safe," said Bruce. "And don't forget to check your helmets." Pointing to one young lad he continued, "You may want to tighten up your chin strap there young man. Okay, you kids go have a good time and we'll see you later." He and Radar moved off and the kids headed down th slope, yelling and laughing with each other.

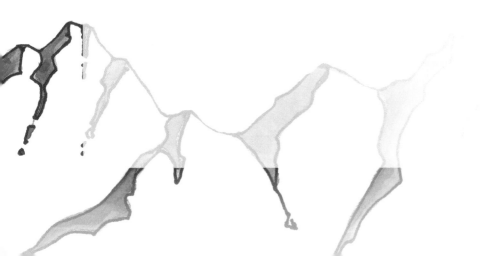

A few hours later, up on Whistler Mountain, another group of older children were having an argument. Chris had come skiing with his sister Kate and their cousin Claudette, who was visiting from Quebec. Chris and Kate didn't see Claudette very often. Claudette loved to ski, but she wasn't used to the size of British Columbia's Coast Mountains. Chris and Kate lived in Whistler and had been skiing since they were small. Now that Chris was twelve years old and Kate was ten, they were allowed to go skiing all by themselves. Claudette was a year older, but she wasn't familiar with the mountain.

They had skied down several of the easier runs, but now Chris wanted to try a new challenge.

"I know where I'm going," he announced. "I've skied here before. I know some great trails that only locals use. Come on, follow me. It'll be fun."

"Chris, I don't think that's such a good idea," argued Kate. "You know darn well Mom and Dad said we were supposed to stay within the ski area boundary. Besides, it's almost one o'clock and we're supposed to meet them in the valley for lunch soon. Remember?"

"So, they'll never know. We'll ski down through the trees and get there in plenty of time. I know the way. It's all right." Chris' voice sounded confident.

"Are you sure?" Claudette asked. "Please don't go too fast. I don't know where I am. These mountains are so huge, it's confusing for me."

"It'll be easy," Chris said again. "I know where to go, come on, you guys, don't be such chickens. Let's have some fun!"

Claudette and Kate looked at each other.

"Don't call us chicken!" Kate gave in. "We can out ski you any day. Just lead the way."

However, when they came to the ski area boundary fence, both girls stopped again.

"Chris, are you sure this is all right?" asked Claudette one final time. She was a year older than Chris, but she knew she didn't know the mountain like he did. "We're not supposed to go past the fence."

"Look, someone else has already gone this way," Chris said, pointing to another set of ski tracks that crossed under the fence. "I've been here before, it's not a problem. Besides, we can just follow those tracks."

"Okay," Claudette said. "I like adventures." She was thinking about the story she would have to tell when she got back to Quebec.

The three of them slipped under the yellow nylon rope and they all ignored the orange plastic disc that read, "SKI AREA BOUNDARY, NO PATROL".

The children followed the ski tracks into the forest, but once inside the trees, the other ski tracks disappeared. Happily the three children continued on through the trees, twisting and turning around Mother Nature's obstacles. This was a lot different than skiing on the clean groomed runs they were used to.

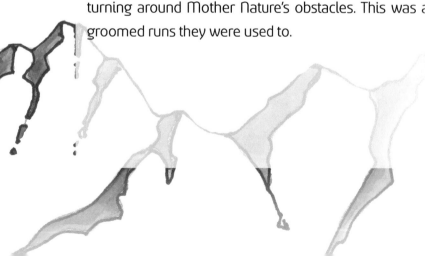

When they all gathered together, Chris appeared concerned. Claudette asked once again, "Chris, are you sure you know where you're going? Maybe we should turn back."

"It's okay," said Chris. "All we have to do is keep going down hill in this direction and we'll come out at the bottom of the chairlift. If we turn back, we'll have to climb back up the hill."

"We should hurry," Claudette said anxiously. "Your parents will be waiting for us."

They went farther and farther down the mountain, but the chairlift didn't appear - instead, they came to the top of a steep cliff.

"Oh, no," Kate said, peering over the edge of the steep black rocks. "We can't get down there. We'll have to go back up the way we came."

"But it's so steep, "Claudette said. "I don't think I can climb up there on skis. I'll have to take my skis off and try to walk."

"That would take forever in this deep snow," Kate answered. Suddenly she got angry, "Chris, this is all your fault. We never should have listened to you."

Chris stared down the steep rocks. He had been so sure he knew where he was going. But turning and twisting through the trees had confused him. He thought he recognized the south side of Blackcomb Mountain through the trees. If that was true, then they were far away from where they were supposed to be.

"I think we should go this way," he said with an uncertain voice. The ski lift must be down there somewhere ... I hope."

"You hope!" yelled Kate.

The mood changed from fun to fear in an instant.

"I'm so hungry," said Claudette.

"And I'm cold," said Kate.

"I've got a chocolate bar," said Chris. "We could each have a piece."

"Great," said Kate. "Hand it over. And then we have to try and figure out how to get out of this mess."

"Maybe the ski patrol will come," said Chris in a small voice. "Remember last week? When Bruce and Radar came to school? He said if we ever got lost, we should wait for them to find us. I think we should stay here and wait."

"I don't think we have a choice," said Kate. "We can't go up, we can't go down. I want Mom and Dad. I'm not going back into that dark forest to get even more lost." Two tears slowly trickled down her cheeks.

"The clouds are moving in," Claudette said. "What if they don't find us and we have to stay here all night? What if there are bears or wolves?"

"The bears are asleep for the winter," argued Chris. "And I've never seen a wolf around here."

"I'm going to sit down and rest," said Claudette, her voice filled with sadness. "I'm so tired and cold. I wish I had never come with you guys."

She took off her skis and put them upside down lengthwise in the snow to sit down on them. Kate took off her skis and sat down beside Claudette.

"Let's sit close together and try to keep each other warm," she said trying to cheer her cousin up. "Come on Chris, you're right, all we can do is wait. Remember, Bruce said if we ever got lost, we had to be smart and not to panic. Now bring out that chocolate bar. I think we need some food to help us keep warm."

The three of them sat down on the skis and stared out over the trees where soon the sun would be setting over the mountains.

Claudette began to cry. "My fingers and toes hurt," she said. "What if we all freeze?"

"Radar and Bruce will find us," Chris said. "Kate is right. We should sit close together and try and keep warm."

Time went slowly by, the sky turned to ash, the trees turned black and a cold wind came blowing towards them – their hope was turning to desperation.

Far below them, on the opposite side of the mountain, Chris and Kate's parents were pacing anxiously at the foot of the mountain. They had been waiting for their children and their niece to show up, but when the children didn't arrive they called the ski patrol.

Bruce and Radar came to meet them. Elaine and Rob MacDonald knew Bruce well. They had all been living in Whistler for years and loved the mountain lifestyle. Rob worked for the municipality in the engineering department and Elaine volunteered at the museum.

They also knew Radar. They knew how hard Bruce was working to train Radar to be a great rescue dog. They were so relieved when they saw them coming towards them.

"When did you last see the kids and what were your exact instructions to them?" Bruce asked.

"We last saw them around nine o'clock this morning, right here. They're allowed to ski by themselves on the green runs. We were all going to meet back here at one o'clock for lunch. They know they are only allowed to ski in certain areas and they have their thirteen-year-old cousin Claudette with them, she's visiting from Quebec," Rob explained making sure he gave Bruce all the facts.

"We haven't had any accident reports involving children this afternoon," Bruce replied. "Do you think they would go outside the ski area boundary?"

"I don't think so," said Elaine. "They know the rules and as you know they've been skiing here since they were little kids."

"Well," said Bruce looking at his watch, "Right now its after two o'clock and the mountain closes in an hour. We'll get a search organized right away. It's going to get dark soon and with these clouds moving in visibility could create a challenge, so there is no time to lose. We'll let you know as soon as we hear anything, keep your cell phones on." He hurried away with Radar trotting beside him.

Bruce and Radar went up the lift immediately. On his way Bruce radioed in the details to Dawn, the ski patrol dispatcher, to get the other ski patrollers organized for when he arrived.

When he arrived at the top of the mountain the professional ski patrollers were waiting outside the alpine maintenance building. Bruce relayed all the facts he knew, "They were last seen at the bottom of the Green Chair around eleven o'clock. Radar and I will check out the Green Chair runs to the east ..."

"I'll hop on the skidoo and search the other runs west of the Green Chair," said Kristine, another senior ski patroller.

Everyone else continued to state where they would search as they all checked their equipment and headed out in pairs. By now it was almost three o'clock, the skies were clouded over, it was getting dark early and many skiers and snowboarders were heading down the mountain to the valley below.

"Okay Radar," said Bruce as he knelt down to eyeball him, "We're on, it's time to work. We're searching for three kids. You know them. Chris and Kate MacDonald and their cousin Claudette."

Radar nodded. The uncanny communication between handler and dog didn't need many words.

Bruce and Radar began to work their way down the ski run.

Radar swept back and forth across the ski run while he listened carefully to Bruce call the kids names.

"Chris, Kate, Claudette ..." They stopped to listen but all they could hear was the faint wind in the trees.

At the bottom of the first pitch, Bruce stopped and called again. Suddenly, Radar's ears perked up and he stopped. His head went up. He gave a short bark.

"What is it, boy?" Bruce questioned, suddenly he saw fresh tracks in the snow beyond the ski area border. "Find them, find the kids, good dog. Search."

Bruce stopped to radio his location to Dawn, who was coordinating the search from the top of the mountain, "Radar found some fresh tracks, it may be them. He's headed into the trees. He seems to have heard something. He seems confident, so we're going in."

"Ten-four," said Dawn. "Kristine, head to Bruce's location and wait on the run."

"Ten-four, on my way," she answered.

Bruce and Radar headed slowly and cautiously into the trees.

"Radar - search," Bruce said. He stopped and called again, "Chris, Kate, Claudette ..." The only reply he got was the wind.

The three kids were now shivering with cold and getting really scared. They had been waiting for almost two hours. Chris had thought help would have arrived a lot sooner. He wondered what his parents did when they didn't show up for lunch. The girls were sometimes angry, sometimes crying. Everything was a mess thought Chris. I'll never do this again he told himself.

It was getting darker and colder. Bruce knew if the kids spent the night outside, it could be very dangerous. He had known them since they were in diapers and he hoped they would apply what he had taught them: to remain where they were and stay together. Fortunately, Bruce knew these trails in the trees. Therefore, if Radar was right and it was the kids, he had a strong idea of where they just may be.

Radar plunged ahead through the snow with Bruce following after him. Out of sight, Bruce heard Radar barking and barking: his pitch increasing with each bark. Then he heard the faint sound of children's voices.

When Bruce made it through the trees to the top of the cliff, he found three shivering children hugging Radar.

"Are you kids all right? Any injuries? Anyone hurt?"

"No, but we are so cold," said Kate, through chattering teeth.

Claudette was in tears and feeling so relieved that help had arrived.

"We'll get you kids out of here right away," Bruce said. He radioed Dawn, "Radar and I have located the children and they're fine but they are very cold and hungry."

"Ten-four Bruce," came the experienced reply.

"Attention all radios ..." Dawn continued with notifying the other patrollers and to make arrangements to get the kids to the valley.

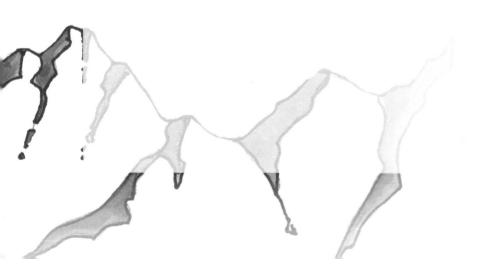

Radar

1977-1986

The MacDonalds were waiting apprehensively below. Dawn had notified them of the meeting point and they were anxiously waiting to see the children. It was after five o'clock now and it was dark. Soon the ski patrollers, Bruce, Radar, and the three children came into sight. Rushing to meet them Elaine and Rob hugged all three children so tight.

"Bruce we can never thank you enough," said teary-eyed Elaine. "What a great team you and Radar are. Thank you everyone for finding them."

"What were you kids thinking?" asked Rob. He had promised himself he wouldn't scold them right away, but he couldn't help himself. " You know you are never supposed to go out of bounds."

"I'm sorry ..." said Chris. "I thought I knew where I was going. I'll never do it again. I promise. It's my fault, don't get angry with the girls. I influenced them and I know that was wrong. I accept responsibility."

"Good for you young man. You kids learned an important lesson today," said Bruce. "We're all just glad that you are okay. I think the sooner you get home, the better."

"Yes, come on," said Elaine. "Into the car with all of you. It's home to hot baths and a big dinner. We'll talk about all this later when we're all rested."

"That we will," said a relieved yet stern Rob.

"They did exactly what I taught them," Bruce explained. "To stay together and to remain in one place. Despite making a bad choice to go out of bounds, you can be proud of their actions, it could have been a lot worse."

Bruce and Radar watched the united family hurry away to the parking lot.

"Good dog, Radar," Bruce said as he leaned down to give him a hug. " Good dog."

He and Radar were tired and cold as well. As they made their way home, Bruce knew that all the hard work of training Radar to be the first civilian avalanche rescue dog in Canada had been worth it. Making sure people were safe on the mountain was the only reward he and Radar wanted.

The Canadian Avalanche Rescue Dog Association

In the late 1970s, Bruce Watt, a professional ski patroller at Whistler Mountain, was caught in an avalanche. Fortunately, he made it out alive. He then approached Whistler Mountain president Franz Wilhelmsen and suggested that the mountain implement a rescue dog program. Franz heartily agreed and he encouraged Bruce to investigate the possibilities.

Bruce tenaciously pursued this by training with Royal Canadian Mounted Police (RCMP) dog handlers in North Vancouver. To be certified he travelled to Banff and Jasper where the RCMP validated the dogs and Parks Canada the handler's mountaineering skills.

Eventually, the RCMP Dog Services supervisors suggested Watt start his own organization; hence, the Canadian Avalanche Rescue Dog Association (CARDA) was founded in 1978. CARDA then developed its own manual, setting standards adopted from the RCMP avalanche dog program: and Radar became the first civilian validated avalanche rescue dog in Canada.

The Canadian Avalanche Rescue Dog Association is a volunteer nonprofit charitable organization. Their goals are to train and maintain a network of highly efficient avalanche search and rescue teams across Canada.

Profits from the sales of Radar the Rescue Dog are being donated to CARDA.

Go to www.carda.ca for more information

Zuzana Riha Driediger

Illustrator

Zuzana Riha Driediger lives in Revelstoke BC, and has been a member of CARDA since 1993. She currently sits on the board of directors for the organization, and helps instruct rescue teams when required. She is presently training her third avalanche rescue dog who looks a lot like Radar. When she is not playing with her dogs in the mountains, Zuzana enjoys drawing and painting.

zuzi-@hotmail.com

Janet Love Morrison

Author

Janet Love Morrison first started skiing on Whistler Mountain in the mid-seventies and years later made the valley her home. During that time she worked for Whistler Mountain Ski Corporation and learnt the concerns surrounding young children getting lost on a mountain. Some rescues were successful; some were fatal. Therefore, she wrote this book with the intent to educate young skiers about mountain and ski safety. Today Love Morrison is a Vancouver based author and editor. Radar the Rescue Dog is her fifth book.

Janet Love Morrison
www.janetlovemorrison.com
janet@janetlovemorrison.com
604.561.2664
Goodwill Ambassador
www.friendstomankind.org

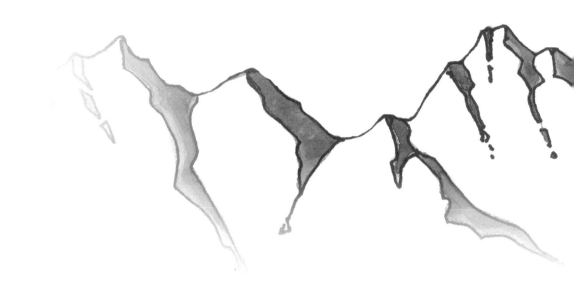

CPSIA information can be obtained
at www.ICGtesting.com
Printed in the USA
LVIW02n0732300913
354376LV00002BA